AF539797

The Book of English Grammar Tenses

MAMTA MEHROTRA

Editorial Support by
IBRAHIM NAMI

Published by

PRABHAT PRAKASHAN PVT. LTD.
4/19 Asaf Ali Road,
New Delhi-110002 (INDIA)
e-mail: prabhatbooks@gmail.com

ISBN 978-93-5562-300-3
THE BOOK OF ENGLISH GRAMMAR TENSES
by Mamta Mehrotra

Edition
2025

Price
₹ 350 (Rupees Three Hundred Fifty Only)

Printed at
SS Japan Arts, Delhi

Author's Note

I am pleased to present this comprehensive grammar book for students, designed to help them master the English language. This book is intended to help students improve their grammar and communication skills.

English grammar can be challenging, but it is essential for effective communication. Whether you are writing an essay, sending an email, or engaging in a conversation, using correct grammar can make all the difference in how your message is received.

Unlike the majority of grammar books currently in the market, this book does not emphasise understanding the definitions of grammatical terms. Instead, an attempt has been made to help the students recognise the tenses and their purpose.

In the examples and exercises, the three different tenses are explained using short and straightforward sentences. The sentences used in the exercises progressively get longer and more complex. The principles have been rationally explained so that the learner can comprehend them with ease.

In this book, you will find clear explanations of grammar rules and numerous examples and practice exercises to help you reinforce your understanding. The book is organised in a logical and easy-to-follow manner, so you can learn at your own pace and track your progress.

Special care has been taken to expose the students to the unique features of English language so that they can avoid committng common errors.

I am grateful to all those who helped me in comprising this book and supported me throughout the process. I would like to give a special thanks to Mr Ibrahim Nami for helping me to edit this book. His efforts have made this book a masterpiece

Hopefully, this book will be a valuable resource for you as you work to improve your grammar skills.

– Mamta Mehrotra

Contents

TENSES

INTRODUCTION

Tense is defined as the form of verb that gives the relation between Time and Action. Time is the duration of work and action is the work done. Tense gives the time when the action is done. There are three phases of time.

The word Tense comes from the Latin word 'tempus' which means time.

(i) Present (time that is now)

(ii) Past (time that has passed)

(iii) Future (time that is yet to come)

Let's consider the sentences given below

(a) Kian eats a mango (Present)

(b) Kian ate a mango (Past)

(c) Kian will eat a mango (Future)

We can observe that each sentence given above has a different meaning. The reason is that each sentence has a different form of verb. Different forms of verbs are called Tenses. The Tense of a verb shows the time of an action or the state of being.

➲ **Read the following sentences.**

1. I write a letter to my principal for availing a day's leave.
2. I wrote a letter to the principal to get approval for a day's leave.
3. I shall write a letter to the principal to get approval for leave, I will be taking.

In sentence 1, the Verb write refers to **present** time.

In sentence 2, the Verb wrote refers to **past** time.

In sentence 3, the Verb shall write refers to **future** time.

Thus a Verb may refer

(1) to **present** time (2) to **past** time, or (3) to **future** time

A Verb that refers to present time is said to be in the Present Tense; as,

I write	I love	I go	I do	I eat

A Verb that refers to past time is said to be in the Past Tense; as,

I wrote	I loved	I went	I did	I ate

A Verb that refers to future time is said to be in the Future Tense; as,

I shall write	I shall love	I shall go	I shall do	I shall eat

Thus there are three main Tenses:

The **Present**, the **Past** and the **Future**.

The Tense of a Verb shows the time of an action or event.

☞ *Note - Sometimes a past Tense may refer to present time, and a present Tense may express future time, as:*

I wish I knew the answer. I'm sorry I don't know the answer. Past Tense - Present time.

Let's wait till he comes. (Present Tense -future time)

Classification of Tenses

There are three Tenses

(i) Present Tense (ii) Past Tense (iii) Future Tense

Each Tense is further divided into four forms. Study the chart given below to understand more about all Tenses and their forms.

❑ TENSE

Present	Past	Future
Indefinite	Indefinite	Indefinite
Continuous	Continuous	Continuous
Perfect	Perfect	Perfect
Perfect Continuous	Perfect Continuous	Perfect Continuous

Below we give the Chief Tense (Active Voice, Indicative Mood) of the verb to go.

Present Tense

	Singular Number	Plural Number
First person	I go	We go
Second person	You go	You go
Third person	He goes	They go

Past Tense

	Singular Number	Plural Number
First person	I went	We went
Second person	You went	You went
Third person	He went	They went

Future Tense

	Singular Number	Plural Number
First person	I shall/will go	We shall/will go
Second person	You will go	You will go
Third person	He will go	They will go

Read these sentences:

1. I go. **(Simple Present)**
2. I am going **(Present Continuous)**
3. I have gone **(Present Perfect)**
4. I have been going **(Present Perfect Continuous)**

The Verbs in all of these sentences refer to the present time, and are therefore said to be in the Present Tense.

In sentence 1, however, the Verb shows that the action is mentioned simply, without anything being said about the completeness or incompleteness of the action.

In sentence 2, the Verb shows that the action is mentioned as incomplete or continuous, that is, as still going on.

In sentence 3, the Verb shows that the action is mentioned as finished, complete, or perfect, at the time of speaking.

The Tense of the verb in sentence 4 is said to be Present Perfect Continuous, because the verb shows that the action is going on continuously, and not completed at this present moment.

Thus we see that the tense of a verb shows not only the time of an action or event, but also the state of an action referred to.

A verb agrees with its subject in number and person. Study the verb forms of various Tenses;

Simple Present Tense	Present Continuous Tense
I speak	I am speaking
You speak	You are speaking
He speaks	He is speaking
They speak	They are speaking

Present Perfect Tense	Present Perfect Continuous Tense
I have spoken	I have been speaking
He has spoken	He has been speaking
We have spoken	We have been speaking
They have spoken	They have been speaking

Simple Past Tense	Past Continuous Tense
I spoke	I was speaking
You spoke	You were speaking
He spoke	He was speaking
They spoke	They were speaking

Past Perfect Tense	Past Perfect Continuous Tense
I had spoken	I had been speaking
You had spoken	You had been speaking
He had spoken	He had been speaking
They had spoken	They had been speaking

Simple Future Tense	Future Continuous Tense
I shall/will speak	I shall/will be speaking
You will speak	You will be speaking
He will speak	He will be speaking
They will speak	They will be speaking

Future Perfect Tense	Future Perfect Continuous Tense
I shall/will have spoken	I shall/will have been speaking
You will have spoken	You will have been speaking
He will have spoken	He will have been speaking
We shall/will have spoken	He shall/will have been speaking
They will have spoken	They will have been speaking

Present Tense

❑SIMPLE PRESENT TENSE (Also called Present Indefinite Tense)

The Simple Present is used:

1. To express a habitual action; as,
   - (a) He drinks tea every morning.
   - (b) I get up every day at five o'clock.
   - (c) My watch keeps good time.
   - (d) I watch television on Sunday.
   - (e) She wakes up every morning at 6 o'clock.
   - (f) He walks in the evening.
   - (g) My shop opens at 9 o'clock.
   - (h) I take exercise every morning.
2. To express general truths; as
   - (a) Plants grow in soil.
   - (b) A magnet attracts iron.
   - (c) Fortune favours the brave.
   - (d) Earth revolves around the sun.
   - (e) Plants give us oxygen.
   - (f) Two and two makes four.
   - (g) Honesty is the best policy.
3. In exclamatory sentences beginning with here and there to express what is actually taking place in the present; as
   - (a) Here comes the bus!
   - (b) There she goes!
   - (c) Here you go!
   - (d) There he goes!
4. In vivid narrative, as substitute for the Simple Past; as,
   - (a) Sohrab now rushes forward and deals a heavy blow to Rustam.

(b) The Sultan hurries to his capital immediately.

(c) Ravana fights bravely but he is killed in the end.

5. To express a future event that is part of a fixed timetable or fixed programme,

   (a) The next flight is at 7 am tomorrow morning.

   (b) The match starts at 9 o'clock.

   (c) The train leaves at 5.20.

   (d) When does the coffee house reopen?

   (e) The school reopens next week.

   (f) The examination commences next month.

☞ *Note also the other uses of the Simple Present Tense.*

1. It is used to introduce quotations; with the verb 'says': as

   (a) Newton says, 'every action has an equal and opposite reaction'.

   (b) Keats says, 'A thing of beauty is a joy forever'.

2. It is used, instead of the Simple Future Tense, in clauses of time and condition; as,

   I shall wait till you finish your lunch.

   If it rains, we will get wet.

3. As in broadcast commentaries on sporting events, the Simple Present is used, instead of the Present Continuous, to describe activities in progress where there is stress on the succession of happenings rather than on the duration.

4. The Simple Present is used, instead of the Present Continuous, with the type of verbs referred to in (221) below.

5. Time clauses and conditional clauses in place of simple future.

   e.g. (a) If you do not earn money, you will not buy the house.

   (b) If you do not work hard, you will fail.

➢ Rules for Affirmative Sentences

Singular subject+ first form of verb+ s/es+.....

Plural subject+ first form of verb+....

e.g. (a) They play cricket on the ground.

(b) She cooks food in the evening.

(c) Water boils at 100°C.

(d) We study in the ABC institution.

(e) She advises me not to smoke.

➢ Rules for Negative Sentences

Singular subject+ does not + first form of verb+.....

Plural subject+ do not+ first form of verb+....

e.g. (a) Kashvi does not watch television.

(b) We do not smoke.

(c) She does not write a letter to her friend.

(d) They do not like to swim.

➢ Rules for Interrogative Sentences

Do/does +subject + first form of verb+..... ?

Question word+ do/does+ subject+ first form of verb+....?

e.g. (a) Do you play cricket?

(b) Does she wash clothes?

(c) Does he not go to school every day?

(d) Why do you weep now?

(e) Whose book do you read?

(f) Whom do you teach?

(g) Which subject does Kashvi not want to study?

(h) Who teaches you English?

(i) Why do you not complete your homework?

Let's Cut A Long Story Short

I play every day. Mother plays with me on Saturday and Sunday.

Kashvi cooks in the morning. Kian washes clothes in the evening.

Jordan plays badminton every day.

Verbs in the simple present tense talk about things that happen regularly or are true in general.

SIMPLE PRESENT TENSE

- Use the simple present to refer to facts and specific routines or habits.
- With state verbs such as think, know, seem, appear, like, consist, have and belong.
- To describe events to make them appear immediate and alive in news headlines and in television, radio, commentary in sports.
- With verbs like promise, agree, assure and demand, which are used to perform the act they describe.

❑ PRESENT CONTINUOUS TENSE

The Present Continuous is used:

1. For an action going on at the time of speaking; as,

   She is singing (now).

   The boys are playing hockey.

2. For a temporary action which may not be actually happening at the time of speaking; as,

   I am reading *'David Copperfield'* (but I am not reading at this moment).

3. For an action that has already been arranged to take place in the near future; as,

   I am going to the cinema tonight.

   My uncle is arriving tomorrow.

It has been pointed out before that the Simple Present is used for a habitual action. However, when the reference is to a particularly obstinate habit - something which persists, for example, in spite of advice or warning we use the Present Continuous with an adverb like always, continually, constantly.

My dog is very silly; he is always running out into the road.

This tense is used in the following ways:

(i) To describe an action in progress and the continuity of the action.

e.g. (a) She is playing tennis.

(b) We are watering the plants.

(c) The passengers are wandering to and fro.

(ii) An action that is not happening at the time of speaking but is in progress.

e.g. (a) He is working in an MNC.

(b) I am teaching in a school.

(c) They are studying in DN College.

(iii) An action that has been pre-arranged to take place in the near future.

e.g. (a) The wedding is going to take place on Sunday.

(b) I am going to attend the class tomorrow.

(iv) Persistent and undesirable habit, especially with adverbs like always, continually, constantly etc.

e.g. (a) You are always running me down.

(b) He is continuously gazing at me.

➢ Rules for Affirmative Sentences

Singular subject+ is/am+ first form of verb+ ing +…..

Plural subject+ are+ first form of verb+ ing+….

e.g. (a) I am playing a game.

(b) She is reading a book.

(c) We are going to Shimla.

➢ Rules for Negative Sentences

Singular subject+ is/am+ not + first form of verb+ ing+…..

Plural subject+ are+ not+ first form of verb+ ing+….

e.g. (a) Kian is not surfing the internet.

(b) They are not watching a movie.

(c) I am not swimming in the water.

➢ Rules for Interrogative Sentences

Is/are/am+ Subject + first form of verb+ ing+….. ?

Question word+ is/are/am + subject+ first form of verb+ ing+….?

e.g. (a) Is Kashvi cooking the food?

(b) Are you not writing a letter?

(c) What is Kashvi doing here?

(d) Which newspaper are you buying?

(e) Why was the camel not drinking water?

 Let's Cut A Long Story Short

Kian is studying. Jordan is brushing his teeth. Their father is reading a newspaper. Nazia and Kashvi are playing badminton. Their coach is watching them play.

Hussain and Abida are flying kites. Abida's kite is flying higher than Hussain's.

Verbs in the present continuous tense talk about an action that is happening at the time of speaking.

Kian is preparing for his exams these days. His brother is helping him revise. Kashvi is visiting the Andamans. She is learning to dive and swim with fish.

Father isn't dropping me to school this month. His bike is giving him trouble.

Verbs in the present continuous tense also talk about an action that is in progress around now but not exactly at the time of speaking. The action has still not finished.

PRESENT CONTINUOUS TENSE

- To refer to activities, situations and changes happenings now/ around now.
- Indefinite adverbs of frequency, always, constantly, forever to refer to regular behaviour which is typical, habitual and predictable, thus it is used to criticize or express disapproval.

SIMPLE PRESENT OR PRESENT CONTINUOUS TENSE

This simple present is much more common than the present continuous, and it is the best form to use if you are not sure.

- The present simple refers to situations which are seen as permanent, and present continuous refers to a situation which we see as temporary.
- When we tell stories we use simple present to describe shorter actions and events and present continuous for longer situations.

- Simple present is used with state verbs, but we can use it with present continuous in an ongoing present process.
- In simple present, see and hear have different meanings -

  I see him every day. (see)

  I see what you mean. (understand)

  I hear you loud and clear. (hear)

  I hear you're coming to stay. (I have been told)

TRY OUT

Fill in the blanks to complete the sentences, using the simple present or present continuous form of the verbs given.

1. Always go
   (a) Kian and I .... to the theatre on Friday.
   (b) I saw Mini in the mall this afternoon she .... shopping!
2. Play
   (a) Arif .... football for a school team.
   (b) Kian .... in goal today because our normal goalkeeper is injured.
3. Have
   (a) I .... lunch at the moment. Can I phone you back in an hour?
   (b) The hotel .... 14 double rooms all with attached bathrooms.
4. Wonder
   (a) We .... if we should buy a birthday present for Kashvi.
   (b) I .... what time the next train is.
5. Come
   (a) Look, here .... the bus, at last!
   (b) More and more people .... to live here these days.
6. (you) think

(a) You look worried, what do .... about?

(b) Why do .... Kian is so happy today? Is it his birthday or something?

7. Stands

(a) The villa .... at the entrance of the hospital.

(b) A strange woman. .... outside the house. Do you know her?

8. Works/Work

(a) At 8:30 on a hot July evening Kian Saxena .... late in his office.

(b) These tablets .... better if you take them with food.

Write three things you are doing at this minute, three things that you are doing, but temporarily, and three things that you always do.

(a) Three things you are doing at this minute.

1. ....

2. ....

3. ....

(b) Three things you are doing these days.

1. ....

2. ....

3. ....

(c) Three things you always do.

1. ....

2. ....

3. ....

KEEP IN MIND

The simple present is much more common than the present continuous.

❑ PRESENT PERFECT TENSE

The Present Perfect is used

1. To indicate completed activities in the immediate past (with just); as, or to express an action that has recently been completed.
   - (a) He has just gone out.
   - (b) It has just struck ten.
   - (c) She has just taken tea.
   - (d) I have purchased a book.
   - (e) They have won the match.
   - (f) He has come now.
2. To describe an action whose time is not given.
   - (a) Have you done MSc in Maths?
   - (b) Have you read Shakespeare?
   - (c) Have you read 'Gulliver's Travels'?
   - (d) I have never known him to be angry.
   - (e) Mr. Kian has been to Japan.
3. To describe past events whose effect still exists.
   - (a) I have finished my work and now I am free.
   - (b) Kashia has eaten all the biscuits (i.e., there aren't any left for you).
   - (c) I have cut my finger (and it is bleeding now).
   - (d) I have finished my work (now I am free).
4. To describe actions that started in the past and are continuing until now and possibly will continue into the future.
   - (a) I have already used this brand of soap.
   - (b) I have known him for a long time.
   - (c) He has been ill since last week.
   - (d) We have lived here for ten years.
   - (e) We haven't seen Kashvi for several months.
5. To show how a past situation relates to the present.

   e.g. I've done my homework, so I can help you with yours now.

The following adverbs or adverb phrases can also be used with the Present Perfect (apart from those mentioned above); never, ever (in questions only), so far, till now, yet (in negatives and questions), already, today, this week, this month, etc.

☞ *Note - The Present Perfect is never used with adverbs of past time. We should not say, for example, 'He has gone to Kolkata yesterday'. In such cases the Simple Past should be used ('He went to Kolkata yesterday').*

➢ Rules for Affirmative Sentences

Singular Subject + has + third form of verb + ...

Plural subject + have + third form of verb + ...

e.g. (a) She has gone to the market.

(b) I have met her.

(c) They have bathed.

(d) It has become dark now.

➢ Rules for Negative Sentences

Singular subject + has + not + third form of verb+ ....

Plural subject +have + not + third form of verb + ...

e.g. (a) I have not called him.

(b) The train has not gone.

➢ Rules for Interrogative Sentences

Has/have+subject+third form of verb + ...?

Question word + has/have +subject + third form of verb + ...?

e.g. (a) Has she gone to Delhi?

(b) Have they not seen the Taj Mahal yet?

(c) What have they eaten today?

(d) Why has the peon not come yet?

 Let's Cut A Long Story Short

Sentences in the present perfect tense talk about an action that happened in the past but has an effect even now. Has or have is used as helping the verb in sentences in the present perfect tense.

PRESENT PERFECT

- It refers to events at an unspecified time in the past which are relevant now.
- Is used to refer to facts, states or development that began in the past and are still continuing or ended a short time ago.
- We refer to past events which we feel are relevant/important.

TRY OUT

Fill in the blanks with just and the present perfect Tense form of the verbs, in the box.

Give, wash, open, have, read, buy, announce, leave, have

1. I am afraid my father is not at home. He has ....
2. There's an article in the paper about our school. Yes, I know I ……….......…… it.
3. I ……………………..…….........……….... my bicycle, so my clothes are wet.
4. My aunt…………………........…......... a new car. She wants to take us for a drive.
5. Why don't we ………………………..........…...dinner in the new restaurant.
6. No l will not have anything. I…………........………....……... my lunch.
7. Anita is very happy. Her company. …………………..her a rise in pay.
8. The principal...........................that we are going to have a holiday tomorrow.

Complete the conversation with present perfect tense.

Ritu: Have you travelled a lot, Hemant?

Hemant: Yes, I have been to four countries.

Anil: Have you been to Sri Lanka?

Hemant: No ....

Rizwan: Have you been to many places in India?

Hemant: Yes, ...

Anita: .... any books of the Harry Potter series?

Hemant: Yes, ...

Preeti : How many times have you read them?

Hemant: ....

KEEP IN MIND

Present perfect describes action in an unspecific time in the past.

❑ PRESENT PERFECT CONTINUOUS TENSE

The Present Perfect Continuous Tense is used for an action which began at some time in the past and is still continuing; as,

(a) He has been sleeping for five hours (and is still sleeping).

(b) They have been building the bridge for several months.

(c) They have been playing since four o'clock.

This Tense is also sometimes used for an action already finished. In such cases the continuity of the activity is emphasized as an explanation of something.

'Why are your clothes so wet? - I have been watering the garden'.

(i) To describe an action that began in the past and is still continuing

(d) They have been staying in the village for a long time.

(e) It has been raining since last night.

(ii) To express an action already completed, but whose effect is still continuing

(f) I have been running around for the job all day and am now tired.

➢ Rules for Affirmative Sentences

Singular subject + has + been + first form of verb + ing + ... + for/since + ...

Plural subject + have +been +first form of verb +ing + for/since + ...

e.g. (a) Kian has been sleeping since 6 o'clock.

(b) They have been running for three hours.

➢ Rules for Negative Sentences

Singular subject + has + not + been + first form of verb + ing+ .... + for since + ...

Plural subject + have +not + been+ first form of verb + ing+ .... + for/since + ...

e.g. (a) You have not been suffering from fever for one week.

(b) Kashvi has not been going to his music class for 2 months.

➢ Rules for Interrogative Sentences

Has/Have + subject + been+ first form of verb +ing + ... + since/for + ... ?

Question word + has /have + subject + been+ first form of verb + ing+ .... + since/for + ...?

e.g. (a) Have you been sleeping since 8 o'clock?

(b) Has he not been living in this house for a long time?

(c) Why have they been playing football since morning?

TIP - We use the Simple Present Tense to describe events that happen in succession, like cricket commentaries, demonstrations of an experiment or asking for and giving instructions. However, the Present Progressive Tense is used for changing and developing situations e.g. Rates of packaged foodstuffs are going up.

WORKSHEET 1

1. **Fill in the blanks with the correct form of present Tense from those given in brackets.**

   (a) I am attempting the Civil Services exam coming up, so I .... (am/is) studying hard these days.

   (b) My grandmother .... (carries/carrying) a walking stick when she goes out for a walk.

   (c) Kian isn't at home. She .... (is/are) out shopping with our father.

   (d) Can you speak louder please, 1 .... (am not/cannot) hear you.

   (e) My widower uncle often .... (coming/comes) to our house for lunch on Sundays.

   (f) Since he changed his job, he .... (found/has found) more time to relax and enjoy his hobby.

   (g) I feel proud of my team as it .... (performed/has performed) very well.

   (h) Look! They .... (gossip and while away/are gossiping and whiling away) their time.

   (i) An apple a day .... (keeps/is keeping) the doctor away.

   (j) By profession, an artist .... (creates/is creating) a picture, whereas an author .... (writes/is writing) a book.

2. **Fill in the blanks in the telephone conversation given below with the correct present Tense form of the verb given in brackets.**

   Kian - Savita! How (a) .... (be) you? This is Sameer.

   Kashvi - Ahhh... Sameer! I (b) .... (be) fine. How are you?

   Kian - I'm great, thanks.

   Kashvi - That (c) .... (be) good. So, what's up?

   Kian - Well, I (d) .... (has) a problem for you to solve.

   Kashvi - Certainly, just say it.

   Kian - My motorcycle (e)......... (be) defective. I (f).......... (try) to repair it for days. I (g).......... (not, know) what is wrong with it. I (h) .... (no, can, fix) it.

WORKSHEET 2

A. Read the sentences given below.

Kian is quite fond of reading books. Every night she reads for at least twenty minutes before going to bed. At times, she narrates these stories to her younger sister. *Alibaba and the Forty Thieves* is Kian's favourite book. However, these days she is reading *Malgudi Days.*

The verbs in bold in the above sentences talk about the present, though in different forms.

☞ **Remember**

- Is' is the Simple Present Tense of the Verb 'be'.
- 'Be' is used as -

I am He/She/ It is We/You/They are

Look at the following table.

Verbs Expressing the Present	
Simple Present (verb + s/es)	**Present Continuous (is/am/are + ing from of the verb)**
1. To talk about habits, routines or actions that are done repeatedly. **e.g.** Shruti goes for her judo classes every evening. 2. To talk about scientific or universal truths. **e.g.** A plant needs air, water and soil to grow. 3. To advise, request and order (imperative sentences). **e.g.** See a doctor at the earliest. Open the book and read the poem.	1. To talk about an action going on at the time of speaking. **e.g.** Shruti is going for her judo classes. 2. To talk about an action going on these days (and not just at the time of speaking). **e.g.** Tarun is learning computers these days.

B. Fill in the blanks in the following passage using the simple present Tense of the verbs given in the brackets.

Yoga **is** (be) a great stress buster. It _______ (help) in improving concentration. It not only _______ (ensure) discipline but also _______ (teach) us how to handle stress levels. It _______ (train) us to channelize surplus energy in a positive manner. Yoga _______ (act) as a magic healer. It _______ (unravel) many hidden qualities that we possess (possess).

C. Imagine yourself to be a TV news reporter. You have been asked to cover a live festival programme going on in the city. Given below is a picture of the festival. Observe the picture and write what various people are doing. One example has been done for you.

Welcome to the live telecast of the City Carnival. On your screen you can see the live coverage of the festival. The Mayor is delivering his speech and his bodyguards are keeping an eye on the crowd.

____

____

____

____

____

____

☞ **Remember**

Present Continuous Tense is used to talk about things that are happening now (at the time of speaking).

WORKSHEET 3

Simple Present or Present Continuous

A. Read the following.

1. I go to the library every weekend.
2. I am going to the library.

Sentence 1 talks about a habitual action, whereas sentence 2 describes an action happening at the time of speaking.

Read this example.

Kashvi **waters** her plants every evening. (habitual action/routine)

However, today she **is watering** them in the morning as she has to go out in the evening (action happening now, at the time of speaking).

☞ **Remember**

Simple Present Tense is used to describe routine/habitual actions/ actions that are happening all the time and not particularly at the time of speaking whereas Present Continuous Tense is used to describe actions happening now, at the time of speaking.

B. Read the passages given below and fill in the blanks with the correct form of the verbs (either simple present or present continuous).

1. Kashvi and Kian are _______ (sit) very quietly in their room. Usually when they are alone, they _______ (make) many mischief, but today they are _______ (wait) patiently for their mother, who has promised to take them for fun rides in the evening. Kashvi is _______ (collect) her books and _______ (arrange) them properly. Kian is _______ (keep) her toys in the rack. She usually _______ (like) to keep them on her bed. Kashvi, too, _______ (prefer) to keep her books on her table but today she is _______ (arrange) them on her bookshelf.
2. Kian _______ (go) for a morning walk every day. He _______ (get) up at 5.30 am and _______ (go) for a brisk walk in a park nearby. He _______ (come) back at 6.30 and _______ (leave) for his school at 7.30. Today he is _______ (think) of reading a book instead of going for his daily walk.

WORKSHEET 4

Non-Action Verbs

A. Read the sentences given below and tick (√) the grammatically correct ones. Give a reason for your choice.

1. I am like this dress. ☐
   I am liking this dress. ☐
2. Kian is wanting to talk with you. ☐
   Kian wants to talk to you. ☐
3. The room freshener smells good. ☐
   The room freshener is smelling good. ☐
4. He knows your dad. ☐
   He is knowing your dad. ☐
5. She owns that house. ☐
   She is owning that house. ☐
6. I hear some noises from the room. ☐
   I am hearing some noises from the room. ☐

☞ **Remember**

♦ Non-Action Verbs, i.e. verbs that do not describe 'an action' are not (or rarely) used in the continuous Tense. \
  For example:
  This soup is tasting sour.
  This soup tastes sour.

♦ Words, such as 'like,' 'want', 'smell', 'know', 'own', etc., are non-action verbs.

The table below gives common non-action verbs.

Verbs Expressing the Present

Verbs of Senses	Verbs of Feelings/ Emotions	Verbs of Mental States	Verbs of Possession
• See • hear • taste • smell	• like • love/hate • feel • want/desire • fear • respect	• know • understand • agree/ disagree • believe • doubt/trust • think • suppose • remember	• own • possess • belong • contain

B. Fill in the blanks with the correct forms of the verbs (simple present or present continuous).

1. Kian _______ (collect) many dry leaves. It is his hobby.
2. Kian is _______ (collect) many dry leaves these days. He has to prepare a Botany project.
3. Hotels in Goa are usually quite expensive. But now they are _______ (slash) their rates because of recession.
4. Software engineers usually _______ (work) for eight hours a day. But on account of the current economic slowdown, they are _______ (work) for over twelve hours a day.
5. Kian _______ (own) this beautiful pencil box.
6. You are _______ (look) fit these days. Are you going (go) to aerobic classes?
7. No, I am not _______ (not go) to any aerobic classes. I just _______ (go) for a morning walk regularly.
8. Is Kashvi ready for school?
   No, she is _______ (have) her bath.

C. Read the following sentences.

1. They **have** a beautiful house.
   ↳ Shows possession

2. They **are having** lunch.
   ↳ Suggests action

Some verbs can be used as both action and non-action verbs. **In Sentence 1**, 'have' shows possession and is, therefore, used as a **'non-action verb'**. **In Sentence 2**, ' are having' suggests that an action is happening, so here, 'have' is an **'action verb'**.

A few more verbs that can be used as both action and non-action verbs are given below. Use them in sentences of your own in both the ways.

1. Think
   - She thought for a moment before answering___(action)
   - I have a thought.________________________(non-action)
2. Feel
   - I am feeling so dizzy.____________________ (action)
   - It is a piece of nylong cloth with a cotton feel (non- action)
   - I have a feeling you will win _________(non-action)
3. Taste
   - Can you taste the garling in the soup?_______ (non-action)
   - She is tasting the soup.__________________ (action)
   - This soup has a bitter taste._________ (non-action)
4. Smell
   - The drain is smelling bad._________________(action)
   - Your hanky has a good smell. _________ (non-action)

Past Tense

❑ SIMPLE PAST TENSE (Also called Past Indefinite Tense)

The Simple Past is used to indicate an action completed in the past. It often occurs with adverbs or adverb phrases of past time.

The steamer sailed yesterday.

I received his letter a week ago.

He left school last year.

Sometimes, this tense is used without an adverb of time. In such cases the time may be either implied or indicated by the context.

I learnt Hindi in Nagpur.

I didn't sleep well (i.e., last night).

Babar defeated Rana Sanga at Khanua.

The Simple Past is also used for past habits; as,

He studied many hours every day.

She always carried an umbrella.

This Tense is used in the following ways;

(i) To indicate an action that happened in the past and to report completed actions. It is used often in recounts and narratives.

(a) We closed the shop at 8 pm.

(b) She met me last year.

(c) I visited the Taj Mahal three months ago.

(d) Once upon a time there lived a one eyed man.

(ii) To indicate past habits or repeated events that are now over.

(a) In those days, my mother gave me some pocket money every day.

(b) I always rode a bike to school when I was young.

(iii) The habitual past can also be expressed by using 'used to'

(a) She used to drink tea in the morning.

(b) My grandfather used to read a few chapters of the Gita every day.

Let's Cut A Long Story Short

I wanted to buy a doll but then I saw a car and liked it more. Grandpa bought me the car. We came home after that. I heard a noise in the afternoon. I went downstairs to check. I looked behind the curtain. I opened and shut the doors. I peeped under the bed. Suddenly, a strong wind blew the window open. A vase fell and broke into pieces. The wind was making the noise!

The verbs in the sentences above are in the simple past tense. They show that something has already happened. The past tense of most verbs is formed by adding - ed or -d to the simplest form of the verb.

Examples: wanted, liked, peeped, opened

❑ PAST CONTINUOUS TENSE

The Past Continuous is used to denote an action going on at some time in the past. The time of the action may or may not be indicated.

- We were listening to the radio all evening.
- It was getting darker.
- The light went out while I was reading.
- When I saw him, he was playing chess.

As in the last two examples above, the Past Continuous and Simple Past are used together when a new action happened in the middle of a longer action. The Simple Past is used for the new action.

This Tense is also used with always, continually, etc. for persistent habits in the past.

- He was always grumbling.

This Tense is used in the following ways.

(i) To indicate an action that was happening at some time in the past. The time of action may or may not be indicated

e.g. We were watching TV the whole evening.

(ii) Used with always, continually, etc., for persistent habits in the past

(iii) The Past Continuous is also used for an action that was going on during a given period or at a period of time in the past.

i.e. While Kian was filling in the hole, his dog was digging another.

➢ Rules for Affirmative Sentences

Singular subject + was+ first form of verb + ing + ...

Plural subject + were + first form of verb + ing + ...

e.g. (a) She was driving her car.

(b) They were making a noise.

➢ Rules for Negative Sentences

Singular Subject + was + not+first form of verb + ing +.......

Plural Subject + were+ not + first form of verb + ing + ...

e.g. (a) She was not singing a song.

(b) They were not behaving nicely .

➢ Rules for Interrogative Sentences

Was/were + Subject +first form of verb + ing + ...?

Question word + was/were +subject +first form of verb + ing + ...?

e.g. (a) Were you eating a mango?

(b) When was the milkman milking the cow?

(c) Why was the blind boy crying?

Let's Cut A Long Story Short

There has been a burglary. Inspector Kamat is asking some questions.

What was happening in the house last evening between 7 and 8 PM? I think I was cooking. No, I am sorry, I was watching a movie. My husband was talking to his friend. My son was driving home. My grandchildren were playing carrom. Their mother was getting ready to go out. Our dog was sleeping.

The verbs in the above sentences tell us what was going on during a particular time in the past. These sentences are in the Past Continuous Tense. Was and were are used as helping verbs in these sentences. We use the -ing form of verbs to show that something was or is happening.

Verbs in the Simple Past Tense tell us about an action or situation in the past which has already happened.

Verbs in the Past Continuous Tense tell us what was going on during a particular time in the past. In the Past Continuous Tense, was and were are used as helping verbs with action verbs in their -ing forms. The verbs in blue tell us what was going on during a particular time in the past.

PAST CONTINUOUS TENSE

- Refers to events which were incomplete or in progress at or around a definite time in the past.
- We use it with words like 'always', 'constantly' and 'forever' signifying repeated past actions. We also use it with 'hope', 'plan', 'think about' and 'wonder' to show uncertainty.
- To make polite suggestions and requests.

SIMPLE PAST OR PAST CONTINUOUS TENSE

- We use 'either'/'both' to talk about two events or situations which happened at or around the same time.
- We use 'either' with verbs like 'hope', 'mean', 'plan' and 'think about' to refer that we intended to do but didn't or can't.

TRY OUT

Fill in the blanks with simple past/past continuous form of the verbs in brackets.

1. .... .that film on TV last night. (you/see)
2. What was that noise last night? Sorry. It was me........................ ....my singing. (practice)
3. I .... last night when suddenly there was a loud bang in the kitchen. (Lie)
4. Kian.. to visit me every single day when I was in hospital. (come)
5. How was the game? Terrible! We ....(lose)
6. After she ...., my mother took to cooking as a hobby. (retire)
7. I ....,why don't you come around for dinner at the weekend? (think)
8. The children.. when l left for work this morning. (still/sleep)
9. What happened to you? Did you cut yourself? Yes, when I................... in the garden this morning. (work)
10. Kian got a job in a factory when he........................... school last year. (leave)

Complete the sentences by putting words and phrases in the correct order with the verb in simple past or past continuous.

1. to invite us/were/they/meaning/but
   They ....kept forgetting.
2. when/he/about/stories/was always/was/telling us
   Our grandfather ....a boy.
3. was/eat/when\/anything/would
   I..a child.
4. side of the road/to/isn't/to drive on the other/getting/but/strange/ I'm/used it.
   It's...it.

5. thinking about/having a barbecue/were/at the weekend/the weather is/if pleasant.
   We...pleasant.
6. From the south of/was constantly/by armies/invaded/being
   The city ....the country.
7. was/your plates/while/one of/the doing/dropped
   Kashvi ....the washing up.
8. heard/as soon as/phoned/her
   I .... the news.
9. what/I said/listening/hear/know you/didn't/because/you weren't to me.
   I ....to me.

Underline the correct options.

1. The police arrested three men who robbed/were robbed a bank at Hazratganj.
2. They planned/were planning to wake up early, but they overslept.
3. I saw Nida in the park today - she read/was reading a book.
4. When she ate/was eating her sandwich, the sun came out.
5. After the film finished/was finishing, I turned the TV off and went to bed.
6. Isha is really shy because everyone criticized/was criticizing her when she was a child.
7. Do you like my watch? My friend gave/was giving it to me for my birthday.
8. My sister is really happy-she passed/was passing all her exams.

KEEP IN MIND

Simple Past is used for events that occurred at a definite time in the past and is over at the time of speaking. And the past continuous is used for events going on at a definite time in the past or for the action that had started but not finished.

❑ PAST PERFECT TENSE

The Past Perfect describes an action completed before a certain moment in the past; as,

- I met him in New Delhi in 1996. I had seen him five years ago.

If two actions happened in the past, it may be necessary to show which action happened earlier than the other. The Past Perfect is mainly used in such situations. The Simple Past is used in one clause and the Past Perfect in the other; as,

- When I reached the station the train had started (so I couldn't get into the train).
- I had finished my exercise when Hari came to see me.
- I had written the letter before he arrived.

This Tense is used in the following ways:

(i) To indicate an action that was completed before a definite time or before another action that took place in the past.

e.g. (a) Kian reached here after you had gone.

(b) The patient had died before the doctor reached the hospital.

(ii) It indicates desires in the past that have not been fulfilled

e.g. I wish I had not wasted my time.

(iii) It expresses those conditions of the past that were impossible to fulfill.

e.g. If you had questioned him earlier things would have improved.

Let's Cut A Long Story Short

We use the Past Perfect Tense:

- To describe an action that has taken place before another action in the past.
- With words like 'already', 'just' and 'before', to refer to the action which is completed before a specific time in the past.
- With indefinite time; words like 'always'.

TRY OUT

Rewrite each sentence, putting one missing word in the correct place.

1. I didn't want to see the film because I seen it already.

....

2. Kashvi and Kian weren't at the party because we invited them.

....

3. Kian felt sick all day so we took him to the doctor.

....

4. They been thinking of going out, but in the end they decided not to.

....

5. Kian had the feeling that he had there before, but he didn't remember when.

....

6. We hadn't waiting very long when someone told us the train had been cancelled.

....

7. Kian had not known anyone like Kashvi before, he was very strange.

....

Complete the sentences using an appropriate past perfect form of the verb in brackets. Sometimes more than one form is possible.

1. Before l bought my flat....... .... a house with friends. (share)
2. .... they were going away for the weekend? (you know)
3. Although he loves football, my brother..........................to see a live match till last weekend. (not go)
4. I can't believe you didn't realize, you................................ ....to turn the gas off. (forgot)

5. Recently he .... of taking a year off and travelling around the world. (think)
6. Kian .... for a couple of hours when he stopped to have some lunch.(write)
7. The speech was so boring people started to leave even before she. .... speaking. (stop)
8. When I went back to my town, I was sad to see that my favourite café.........................….(close down)

KEEP IN MIND

Past perfect describes an action that is completed in the past.

❑ PAST PERFECT CONTINUOUS TENSE

The Past Perfect Continuous is used for an action that began before a certain point in the past and continued up to that time.

This Tense is used in the following way:

e.g. (a) When we met in Lucknow she had been studying in City College for three years.

(b) At that time, he had been working in the company for two months.

➢ Rules for Affirmative Sentences

Subject+ had been + first form of verb + ing+ .... + since/ for + ...

e.g. (a) You had been suffering from fever since Tuesday.

(b) I had been studying for three hours.

➢ Rules for Negative Sentences

Subject + had + not+been + first form of verb +ing + ... + since/for + ...

e.g. They had not been going to office since the 5th of July

➢ Rules for Interrogative Sentences

Had + subject + been + first form of verb + ing + ... + since/for + ...?

Question word + had + subject + been + first form of verb + ing + ... since/for + ...?

(a) Had you not been reading the book since morning?

(b) Where had he been playing since morning?

WORKSHEET 5

Read the sentences given below.

I **missed** my bus and **reached** the office late. My boss **was fuming** with anger. He **had** already **assigned** my work to a colleague.

The verbs in bold in the above sentences talk about the past.

Look at the table given below

Verbs Expressing the Past					
Simple Past	Past Continuous	Past Perfect	Present Perfect	Present Perfect Continuous	Past Perfect Continuous
(Past Tense of the verb) (prayed, wrote)	(was/were+ing form of the verbs) (was/were praying, was/ were writing)	(had+past participle form of the verb) (had prayed, had written)	(has/ have+ past participle form of the verb) (has/have, prayed, has/have written)	(has/have+ been+ing form of the verb) (has/ have been praying, has/ have been writing)	(had+ been+ ing form of the verb) (had been praying, had been writing)
1. To talk about an action that took place at some point in the past. e.g. I **bought** this dress yesterday. 2. To talk about a past habit. e.g. He **went** to the church every Sunday.	1. To talk about action that was going on at some point in the past. e.g. The teacher **was checking** the notebooks. 2. To talk about frequently repeated past action. e.g. She **was always complaining** about the system. 3. To express the gradual development of an action e.g.The listeners **were becoming** impatient.	1. To talk about an action already completed before a certain point in the past. e.g. He **had learnt** his lesson before the eighth period.	1. To talk about an action just completed. e.g. I **have talked** to the Principal. 2. To talk about an action that happened in the past but whose effect can be felt at the moment of speaking. e.g. I **have read** all these books(so I need not read them now.)	1. to talk about an action that began in the past, is continuing at the time of speaking and will extend into the future. (We use 'since', 'for' with this Tense). e.g. Riya **has been playing** for two hours now. Ishu **has been staying** in Delhi since 2010.	1. To talk about an action that began before a specific moment in the past, had continued up to that moment and was still in progress. e.g. My teacher **had been teaching** for nearly half an hour when I reached the class

WORKSHEET 6

A. Fill in the blanks with the simple past tense of the verbs given in the brackets.

Long ago, there ______ (be) a forest full of trees laden with ripe, juicy guavas, mangoes, apples and pears. But the birds which lived (live) there were unhappy. They ______ (want) to eat grains. One morning, the birds ______ (see) several grains scattered on the ground. They ______ (sit) down to eat the grains. Suddenly, two bird catchers ______ (rush) out from the nearby bushes and ______ (throw) a huge net on the birds feeding on grains.

☞ **Remember**

Simple Past is used to express an action that happened in the past.

B. Fill in the blanks with the past continuous tense of the verbs given in the brackets.

1. It ______ (rain) heavily and Kian ______ (sneeze)continuously. Mother ______ (make) herbal tea for him. I ______ (try) to concentrate on my work but Kian's loud sneezing ______ (disturb) me.
2. As a child, Kashvi ______ always ______ (complain) about one thing or the other.
3. The day ______ (get) brighter and Kashvi ______ still ______ (sleep) in her bed. She was in fact snoring (snore).
4. The minister ______ (deliver) his speech, but people ______ hardly ______ (listen). Some of them ______ (talk) to one another while others ______ simply ______ (enjoy) a quick nap. Clearly, the speech was not interesting at all.

☞ **Remember**

Past Continuous Tense is used to talk about actions that were in progress at a point of time in the past.

WORKSHEET 7

❑ SIMPLE PAST OR PAST CONTINUOUS

A. Read the following.

1. I painted my room yesterday.
2. I was painting my room at 5.00 PM yesterday.

In Sentence 1, the action was completed in the past.

In Sentence 2, the action (of painting) was in progress at some point of time in the past.

☞ **Remember**

Simple Past is used to express a completed past action whereas **Past Continuous** is used to express an action that was going on at some point of time in the past. These two Tenses are often used together to show that one action was going on when another action happened.

e.g. I **was doing** my homework when the lights **went** off.

↓ action 1 was in progress ↓ action 2 happened

B. Fill in the blanks using the correct Tense – either simple past or past continuous - of the verbs given in the brackets.

1. Kashvi __________ (drop) her purse accidentally while she __________ (board) the metro.
2. I __________ (tell) a story to my daughter when the guests __________ (arrive).
3. When the thief __________ (realise) that the policeman ______ (look) at him, he __________ (run) away.
4. Just as I __________ (go) out of the office, it started raining.
5. My fever __________ (get) worse, so I ______ (go) to a doctor.
6. Kashvi __________ (fracture) her hand while she __________ (holiday) in Jaipur.
7. I __________ (see) the Eiffel Tower when I __________ (stay) in Paris.
8. When the Principal __________ (come into the class, everybody __________ (make) mischief. The girls __________ (sing) songs loudly and the boys __________ (make) paper balls.

WORKSHEET 8

Fill in the blanks with the present perfect tense of the verbs given in the brackets.

1. My parents ____________ (agree) to send me to the picnic.
2. The teacher ____________ (call) my parents for a meeting.
3. Vikram ___(get) a new computer. He can work much faster now.
4. Rahul ________ (fall) from the stairs. We must take him to a doctor.
5. Prices of the basic commodities ________ (rise) sharply over the last two months, Though the government ___ (take) many measures to control the situation.
6. ____________ you ____________ (find) your mobile phone?
   No ____________ you ____________ (see) it anywhere?
7. I ____________ (finish) my homework. Now can I come with you to the mall?
8. I ______________ (stay) in this hotel twice. It has really spacious rooms.

Remember

Present Perfect Tense is used to express –

- an action recently completed.
- an action that was completed in the past but whose effect can be felt at the time of speaking.

WORKSHEET 9

❑ SIMPLE PAST OR PRESENT PERFECT

A. Read the following.

1. I called the plumber to fix the leaking water pipe.
2. I have called the plumber to fix the leaking pipe.
   He may arrive any moment.

Sentence 1 talks about an action in the past that has no connection with the present.

Sentence 2 talks about a past action that is linked with the present.

(Action—have called the plumber) (connection with the present – he may arrive any moment)

☞ **Remember**

If a past action has a link with the present, we use Present Perfect. If a past action has no link with the present, we use Simple Past. Also remember that we do not use any past time reference, such as 'yesterday', 'last week', etc., with Present Perfect Tense.

B. Some verbs in the sentences given below have been used in wrong forms. Underline them and write the correct forms. One has been done for you.

1. I <u>have met</u> him yesterday.
   I met him yesterday.
2. I knew him since his childhood.
3. Various new inventions and discoveries by our scientists made our lives extremely comfortable.
4. The Delhi metro made commuting a comfortable experience for the people.
5. Dr. Laennec of France has invented the stethoscope in 1816.
6. The invention of the stethoscope has actually happened accidentally.

7. The state government built 7 new flyovers recently to tackle the increasing traffic. The officials hope these will save at least 30 minutes of travel time.

C. Fill in the blanks with either simple past or present perfect Tense of the verbs given in the brackets.

BREAKING NEWS

1. The famous industrialist Mr. Kapoor __________ (donate) Rs 50 lakhs to an orphanage. Mr. Kapoor __________ (hand) over the cheque to the Manager of the orphanage this morning. Mr. Kapoor __________ (made) many such donations in the past.
2. Mr. Sharma of Delhi __________ (become) the first person to walk through the entire nation on foot. It __________ (take) him four years to complete this feat.
3. The government __________ (declared) Monday a public holiday on account of the sudden demise of the minister. The minister __________ (die) of a heart attack.

WORKSHEET 10

A. Fill in the blanks with Past Perfect Tense:

I _____________ (promise) my baby sister that I would take her to the Children's Park if she behaved well throughout the day. When I got back in the evening, I was pleasantly surprised to see that my sister _____________ (cleaned) her room perfectly. She _____________ (put) her books in the bookrack. She _____________ (change) the bed sheet. She _____________ (finish) her homework and _________ even _____________ (learn) her science lesson. Mother told me that she _____________ (help) in the kitchen too. I was impressed. Since she _____________ (keep) her word, I decided to keep my promise too.

☞ **Remember**

Past Perfect Tense is used to talk about an action completed before a given moment in the past.

e.g When **I reached home**, she **had already cleaned the room**.

↓ action 2 ↓ action 1

Past Perfect	**Past**	
Action 1	**Action 2**	**Time of speaking**

WORKSHEET 11

SIMPLE PAST OR PAST PERFECT

A. Read the following.

1. I painted my room.
2. I **had painted** my room before **the guests arrived**.

↓ Action 1 ↓ Action 2

Remember

We use Simple Past to express an action that happened in the past. We use **Past Perfect** when one past action was completed before another past action.

Past
←

____Time of speaking

I painted my room. The guests arrive.

B. Complete the following story using either Simple Past or Past Perfect Tense of the verbs given in the brackets.

Brave Kashvi

Kashvi was a very clever girl who always ______ (study) hard and ______ (obey) her elders. One day, when her mother ______ (go) to the market, Kashvi ______ (sit) down to do her homework. Suddenly, she ______ (smell) smoke. When she ______ (look) out of the window, she ______ (see) that there was a fire in her friend's house. Her friend's family ______ (go) out of station. Kashvi ______ (think)fast. She ______ (remember) that her teacher ______ (teach) her a lesson on useful services, such as the police station, fire brigade, hospital, etc. She ______ (know) the phone number of the fire brigade well because her father ______ (make) her remember these numbers. Kashvi quickly ______ (call) the fire station and ______ (request) for help. The fire engine ______ (arrive) quickly and put out the fire. Everybody in the neighbourhood ______ (praise) Kashvi.

WORKSHEET 12

A. Read the following.

1. We **have been waiting** for the bus **for** two hours now. Why has the bus not reached yet?
2. Rohit **has been looking** for a job since January.

☞ **Remember**

Present Perfect Continuous Tense is used to express an action that began in the past, is in progress at the time of speaking and will continue for some time in the future (or has just ended).

B. Observe your friends around you. Now write a few things that they have been doing

1. Tina has been talking to Rakhi since the first period.
2. ________________________________
3. ________________________________
4. ________________________________
5. ________________________________
6. ________________________________

WORKSHEET 13

❑ PRESENT CONTINUOUS OR PRESENT PERFECT CONTINUOUS

A. Read the following sentences.

1. Manasvi is dancing.
2. Manasvi has been dancing for over one hour now.

In Sentence 1, the emphasis is on the present aspect of the action.

In Sentence 2, the emphasis is on the period/duration for which the action has been in progress.

☞ **Remember**

We use -

- Present Continuous to talk about an action going on at the moment of speaking.
- Present Perfect Continuous when we want to mention when an action started or for how long it has been in progress.

B. Complete the following with either Present continuous or Present Perfect Continuous forms of the verbs given in the brackets.

1. He ______ (write) a book these days.
   He ______ (write) it for over a year now.
2. Please go inside the Manager's office.
   He ______ (wait) for you since morning.
3. Social evils, such as child marriage and dowry system, ______ (harm) our country for centuries.
4. They ______ (live) here since 2004.
5. The tenant who ______ (live) here these days is a journalist.
6. The company ______ (won) this trophy every year since 2011.
7. The company ______ (compete) for this trophy for the third consecutive time.
8. I ______ (play) a lot of chess these days.

9. Deepa ______ (prepare) for her recitation competition. She ______ (rehearse) for more than three hours.

10. She ______ (work) with this company since January. She ______ (work) as a Senior Software Engineer.

WORKSHEET 14

1. Fill in the blanks with the correct form of past tense by selecting from the options given in brackets.

(a) The other employees had already left the office but Kashvi .... (still worked/was still working) there.

(b) A small boy .... (fell/was falling) from the train when it was moving at full speed.

(c) We saw a bus fallen into a ditch when we .... (went/were going) to Mussoorie.

(d) Anita .... (burnt/was burning) her finger while she was cooking.

(e) While I .... (waited /was waiting) for my bus Rachita was running after hers.

(f) The farmer sold the crop after he .... (harvested/had harvested) it.

(g) Indians .... (had fought/fought) a long struggle before they .... (had attained / attained) independence.

(h) The train .... (departed/had departed) before we reached the station.

2. Fill in the blanks with the correct form of past tense of the verbs given in brackets.

(a) Binod ...... (bring up) by his father because his mother died when he was a baby.

(b) Rarnesh, who .... (work) in Kolkata for 10 years, is now seriously ill.

(c) I once .... (hear) Honey Singh singing live on the stage.

(d) Majid, my best friend, ... (stay) in Kanpur for the last five years.

(e) Kritika .... (break) her left ankle bone while she .... (dance) at the party.

(f) Tailor Master, are the clothes I .... (give) for stitching ready yet?
(g) Parveen .... (not/write) a letter to me since last year.
(h) Mummy, tell Papa that his phone .... (ring) while he .... (have) his bath.

Future Tense

❑ SIMPLE FUTURE TENSE (also called Future Indefinite Tense)

This Tense is used in the following ways

(i) To say what we believe or think will happen in future.

e.g. (a) I believe she will join the office tomorrow.

(b) They will go to college.

(c) We will win the match.

(ii) Things which we cannot control and are factum

e.g. The sun will rise at 6:00 am.

(iii) To indicate an instant decision.

e.g. It is our first marriage anniversary. I will give you a precious gift.

➢ **Rules for Affirmative Sentences**

♦ You/He/She/lt/They (Second and Third Person Pronouns)+ will+ first form of verb + ...

♦ I/We (First Person Pronouns) + shall + first form of verb+ ....

e.g. (a) We will sell his house.

(b) I will purchase a new car.

➢ **Rules for Negative Sentences**

♦ You/He/She/lt/They (Second and Third Person Pronouns) + will + not + first form of verb + ...

♦ I/We (First Person Pronouns) + shall + not + first form of verb + ...

e.g. (a) We shall not leave the exams.

(b) My friend will not host dinner this evening.

➢ **Rules for Interrogative Sentences**

- Will/shall+ subject + first form of verb +......?
- Question word + will/shall + subject + first form of verb + ...?

e.g. (a) Will she not come to the party?

(b) Who will help him?

(c) Why will your friend not come here?

Let's Cut A Long Story Short

Sentences that talk about things that will take place in the future are in the simple future tense.

We use will or shall to speak about events that happen in future. Shall is rarely used these days.

Will also shows that you have decided to do something. Shall is used to ask if something is a good idea or to suggest what can be done. It is used with I and we.

❑ FUTURE CONTINUOUS TENSE

This tense is used in the following ways.

(i) To indicate an action that will occur in the normal course.

e.g. (a) She will be cooking the food tomorrow.

(b) I will be meeting him tomorrow.

(ii) To indicate an action that will be in progress at a given point of time in the future.

e.g. (a) At this time tomorrow, we shall be attending the party.

(b) We shall be visiting the zoo at this time tomorrow.

➢ **Rules for Affirmative Sentences**

- ♦ You/He/she/it/They (Second and Third Person Pronouns) + will+ be + first form of verb + ing + ...
- ♦ I/We (First Person Pronouns) + shall + be + first form of verb +ing + ...

e.g. (a) I shall be teaching my students.

(b) Next year my teacher will be going to China.

➢ **Rules for Negative Sentences**

- ♦ You/He/she/it/They (Second and Third Person Pronouns)+ will + not +be + first form of verb+ ing + …..
- ♦ I/We (First Person Pronouns)+ shall + not +be + first form of verb+ ing + …..

e.g. (a) They will not be studying in City College.

(b) I shall not be bathing this evening.

➢ **Rules for Interrogative Sentences**

- ♦ will/shall + subject + be + first form of verb+ ing +.....?
- ♦ Question word + will/shall + subject + be + first form of verb+ ing +.....?

e.g. (a) Will this boy be wandering in the forest?

(b) How long will they be travelling?

FUTURE PERFECT TENSE

This Tense is used to describe an action which will be completed at some point of time in the future.

e.g. (a) I shall have finished this work by tomorrow.

(b) They will have reached home by now.

(c) I shall have reached the school before the bell rings.

➢ Rules for Affirmative Sentences .

- You/He/She/It/They (Second and Third Person Pronouns) + will + have + third form of verb + ...
- I/We (First Person Pronouns) + shall + have + third form of verb + ...

e.g. (a) We shall have cooked the food by the evening.

(b) Your examination will have been over by Tuesday.

➢ Rules for Negative Sentences

- You/He/she/It/They (Second and Third Person Pronouns) + will + not + have + third form of verb + ...
- I/We (First Person Pronouns) + shall+ not + have + third form of verb + ...

e.g. (a) I shall not have written the letter by noon.

(b) The passengers will not have reached the station before the train starts.

(c) Your brother will not have read this novel before next Saturday.

➢ Rules for Interrogative Sentences

- Will/shall + subject + have + third form of verb +.....?
- Question word + will/shall + subject + have + third form of verb ......?

e.g. (a) Will he not have gone before I get there?

(b) What will he have eaten before he sleeps?

❑ FUTURE PERFECT CONTINUOUS TENSE

This tense is used in the following way.

It describes an action that will be in progress over a period of time that will end in the future.

e.g. (a) At noon Anuradha will have been singing songs for an hour.

(b) I will have been working round the clock for twenty - two years next April.

➢ **Rules for Affirmative Sentences**

♦ You/He/She/lt/They (Second and Third Person Pronouns) +will + have + been + first form of verb + ing + ...

♦ I/We (First Person Pronouns) + shall + have + been + first form of verb + ing + ...

e.g. By next April we shall have been leaving for the USA.

➢ **Rules for Negative Sentences .**

♦ You/He/She/lt/They (Second and Third Person Pronouns) + will + not + have + been + first form of verb + ing + ...

♦ I/We (First Person Pronouns) + shall + not + have + been + first form of verb + ing + ...

e.g. (a) I shall not have been writing for half an hour.

(b) Mahima will not have been going to Kanpur for a long time.

➢ **Rules for Interrogative Sentences**

♦ Will/shall + subject + have + been + first form of verb + ing + ...? .

♦ Question word + will/shall + subject + have + been + first form of verb + ing + ...?

e.g. (a) Will she have been playing for some time?

(b) Why will you not have been going to school since 8 o'clock?

Let's Learn

We use future time in many ways.

- Expresses personal intention or action taking place in the immediate future.
- Expresses probability
- Expresses future plans and arrangements
- Expresses future action which are determined in advance by a calendar, a timetable or programme

} Present Continuous
Simple Present

- Expresses an offer or request
- Expresses future fact or prediction

} Will/Shall+ Verb

TRY OUT

Write replies to these people which are true to you. Use the future forms.

1. What are your plans for the next weekend?

   ....

2. What do you think the main change in your town will be in the next five years?

   ....

3. Tell me what ideas you've had for improving your English skills in the next few weeks?

   ....

4. What is the weather forecast for the next few days?

   ....

5. What were your friends doing for a holiday this year?

   ....

6. How do you see your next few years, from your study point of view?

   ....

7. May be we can arrange to meet for a walk, what is your plan tomorrow evening?

   ....

8. Thanks for inviting me for dinner tonight, what's on the menu?

   ....

9. Do you know of an interesting place in your city, where things are happening in the next few days?

   ....

A. Complete the dialogues using appropriate future forms of verbs in brackets.

1. a. It's going to be a really boring party.

   b. No, Nasir ....and he's always good fun.(go)

2. a. I'm sorry, we've run out of chicken.

   b. Oh, all right I... mutton then, please. (have)

3. a. Why do you need a new laptop?

   b. My old one's very old and it. .... work one of these days. (stop)

4. a. Do you need help to look after the children tonight?

   b. No, it's ok. They ....with my mother. (stay)

5. a. It's a bit hot in here isn't it?

   b. Just a second. I. ....the window. (open)

6. a. Have you got a hammer I can borrow?

   b. No, Sorry. Ask Qazi I bet he. ....you one. (lend)

7. a. Do you want to play tennis this afternoon?

   b. I can't. I... .... my sister to the airport. (take)

8. a. I've got an appointment with Dr. Patel.

   b. That's fine. Take a seat and we .... you when she's fine. (call)

B. Complete the dialogues using appropriate future forms of the verb in brackets.

1. a. ....? (be)

   b. On April 22, She'll be 13.

2. a. ....? (arrive)

   b. Half past three. As long as its on time.

3. a. ....? (snow)

   b. No, I don't think so. It hardly ever snows here.

4. a. ....? (do)

   b. I'm going to have dinner with some friends.

5. a. ....? (have)

   b. Probably pasta or something like that.

6. a. ....?(win)

   b. The next election? No idea! I hate politics?

7. a. ....? (buy)

   b. I'm not sure. May be a book, because I know she likes reading.

8. a. ....? (stay)

   b. No, with some friends actually. They live right next to the beach.

KEEP IN MIND

Will is the most common in referring to future time.

WORKSHEET 15

1. Fill in the blanks with the correct form of future Tense of the verbs given in brackets.

(a) Now Nikhil......(want) to move to a bigger city for a better job.

(b) The famous Dr. Prahlad .... (operate) on my uncle tomorrow to remove his tumour.

(c) Sarla's mother .... (stay) in a rented house after her divorce gets through.

(d) Prodipta .... (win) the wrestling bout against Vijay this evening, I'm sure.

(e) I think Ranjan .... (start) his journey tomorrow.

(f) Our Maths teacher ....(correct) the exam papers by Sunday.

(g) I think Anil .... (certainly/get) good marks in the Social Science test.

(h) By 7 pm, Sameera .... (finish) her homework.

2. Fill in the blanks with the correct form of future Tense by selecting from the options given in brackets.

(a) The train .... (will have left/ will leave) from Rajkot by 10 pm.

(b) My grandfather will .... (have arrived/be arriving) at home by now.

(c) The entertainment programme .... (will have ended/will end) by now.

(d) I think that tomorrow Ramita .... (is start) on her new project.

(e) My class teacher .... (probably assigning / will probably assign) a lot of homework for the summer holidays.

(f) The building contractor .... (will finishing/ will be finished) my new house by next month.

(g) I will .... (be completing/have completed) the task at this time tomorrow.

(h) I .... (will be passing/will have passed) my MBA by the time you return from abroad.

3. Fill in the blanks with the correct form of the verb (mixed Tenses) given in brackets.

One day a husband and wife

(a) ...... (drive) to the countryside to visit their friends when they realized they needed to stop for petrol. The man was filling up the car when he

(b) ...... (see) a penguin standing at the petrol pump. He

(c) ...... (think) it was very strange and when he went to the cashier to pay. he asked, "Why is there a penguin standing next to the pump?" The cashier replied, "'I don't know It

(d) .... (be) there all morning."

EXERCISE IN COMPOSITION

Choose the correct verb form from those in brackets.

1. The earth ________ round the sun. (move, moves, moved)
2. My friends ________ the Prime Minister yesterday. (see, have seen, saw)
3. I ________ him only one letter up to now. (sent, have sent, send)
4. She ________ worried about something. (looks, looking, is looking)
5. It started to rain while we ____________ tennis. (are playing, were playing, had played)
6. He __ fast when the accident happened. (is driving, was driving, drove)
7. He __asleep while he was driving. (falls, fell, has fallen)
8. I'm sure I __ him at the party last night. (saw, have seen, had seen)
9. He ______ a mill in this town. (have, has, is having)
10. He ___ here for the last five years. (worked, is working, has been working)

11. He thanked me for what I _____ . (have done, had done, have been doing)
12. I ______ a strange noise. (hear, am hearing, have been hearing)
13. I ____ him for a long time. (know, have known, am knowing)
14. I _____ English for five years. (study, am studying, have been studying)
15. Don't disturb me. I ______ my homework. (do, did , am doing)
16. Kian ________ to be a doctor. (want, wanting, is wanting)
17. The soup ______ good (taste, tastes, is tasting)
18. He ______ TV most evenings. (watches, is watch, is watching)
19. He ______ out five minutes ago. (has gone, had gone, went)
20. When he lived in Hyderabad, he _____ to the cinema once a week. (goes, went, was going)
21. The baby ____ all morning. (cries, has been crying)
22. I ________ Rahim at the zoo. (saw, have seen, had seen)
23. I ___ Kumar this week. (haven't seen, did't see, am not seeing)
24. This paper ______ twice weekly. (is appearing, appearing, appears)
25. Kian fell off the ladder when he _______ the roof. (is mending, was mending, mended)

EXAM PRACTICE

Error Correction

Each of the following sentences in this exercise has an underlined word/phrase and three words/phrases are given after the sentence. If one of the given words/ phrases makes the sentence grammatically correct, select the word/phrase as your answer. If the sentence is grammatically correct as it is, choose option (d), i.e. No correction.

1. When Kovid died he and Nisha <u>had been</u> married for six years.
   (a) have been (b) has been
   (c) having been (d) No correction

2. If it <u>rained</u> we <u>will</u> get wet.
   (a) rains, will be (b) raining, will
   (c) rains, will (d) No correction

3. I am <u>contribute</u> to my nation's infrastructure.
   (a) contributing (b) contributed
   (c) contributes (d) No correction

4. I <u>appeared</u> for the interview today.
   (a) appear (b) has appeared
   (c) appearing (d) No correction

5. In the last ten years, the problem <u>has almost became</u> an epidemic.
   (a) becomes (b) become
   (c) had become (d) No correction

6. She <u>waiting</u> for her sister's marriage.
   (a) waits (b) is waiting
   (c) will waiting (d) No correction

7. Digital downloads <u>having</u> changed the way we listen to music.
   (a) been (b) having been
   (c) have (d) No correction

8. Now would be a good time to <u>got</u> your stuff in order.
   (a) get (b) getting
   (c) gets (d) No correction

9. Sunil <u>will have arrived</u> in the hospital by now.
   (a) has arrived (b) is arriving
   (c) will has arrived (d) No correction

10. But nothing has changed in the way we are storing and manage our MP3s.
    (a) managed (b) manages
    (c) managing (d) No correction

11. Kejriwal puts 18 conditions before Sonia and Rajnath.
    (a) put (b) putting
    (c) had puts (d) No correction

12. Bru Gold coffeee have an incredible aroma.
    (a) having (b) has
    (c) had (d) No correction

13. I have read this book since 10 am.
    (a) have been read (b) have reading
    (c) have been reading (d) No correction

14 Does Sakshi go for a walk every morning?
    (a) goes (b) going
    (c) will go (d) No correction

15. Samir came to meet me after you have leaving.
    (a) have left (b) had left
    (c) left (d)No correction

16. As soon as Meena heard the alarm, she left for work.
    (a) hears (b) hear
    (c) will hear (d) No correction

17. Watching too many cartoons and junk food consumption are triggers that are lead to obesity in children.
    (a) are lead (b) lead
    (c) are leading (d) No correction

18. When I left home my brother watch television.
    (a) watches (b) watched
    (c) was watching (d) No correction

19. The earth revolved around the sun.
    (a) revolves (b) is revolving
    (c) revolve (d) No correction

20. All of us have a great time at the party.
    (a) had (b) will having
    (c) having (d) No correction

Editing Tasks

The following passage has not been edited. There is an error in each of the lines against which a blank is given. Write the incorrect word and the correction in the space provided. Remember to underline the word that you have supplied.

1.

	Incorrect	Correct
(a) When Gagarin has been in space for over an hour, he had	....	....
(b) nearly complete a journey right round	....	....
(c) the Earth and it is time to prepare	....	....
(d) for the landing. If he come into the	....	....
(e) air too quickly, his ship will rub against	....	....
(f) the air particles and the friction will make	....	....
(g) the ship so hot that it would burnt up	....	....
(h) The speed of the Vostok had to be check gradually	....	....

2.

	Incorrect	Correct
On a pleasant holiday morning, the residents of		
(a) Sunny's and Aditi's neighbourhood meeting at	....	....
(b) the park. Each family had bring something	....	....
(c) to eat. There were a variety of dishes	....	....
(d) The picnickers has a delicious treat of food.	....	....
(e) Food are one of our basic necessities.	....	....

(f) It is the fuel that gave us energy ……….. ………..

(g) People live near the sea coast ……….. ………..

(h) eats a lot of fish. ……….. ………..

Omission Task

In the following passage, one word has been omitted in each of the lines, against which a blank is given. Write the missing word along with the word that comes before and the word that comes after it in the space provided. Remember to underline the word you have supplied.

1.

	Before	Missing	After
(a) A bookshop not something	………	………	………
(b) you in every gali or mohalla	………	………	………
(c) these days. Books, which once a staple diet for youngsters in their	………	………	………
(d) formative years, fading out of their list of engagements.	………	………	………
(e) Ask any youngster which the	………	………	………
(f) latest book he read and	………	………	………
(g) he will baffled. A seventeen year	………	………	………
(h) old school-goer says that he just his Physics book.	………	………	………

Reordering of Sentences

Rearrange parts of the sentence in the correct order.

1. P: the complete course

   Q: is of three

   R: of a graduate degree

   S: years duration

   (a) PRQS (b) PQRS (c) SQRP (d) SRQP

2. P : the duration of the course

   Q : please let me know

R : as well as

S : the total fees

(a) QRSP (b) QPRS (c) SRPQ (d) SRQP

3. P : your advertisement

Q : in the Times of India

R : of 16th July

S : I came across

(a) SPQR (b) SRQP (c) RSQP (d) RQSP

4. P : and is extremely

Q: my son is

R : good looking

S : eight years old

(a) PQRS (b) PRSQ (c) QSPR (d) QPRS

5. P : the whole idea of

Q : majority and minority

R : in India

S : is irrelevant and inappropriate

(a) PRQS (b) PQRS (c) SRQP (d) PQSR

6. P : look is terms

Q: one must also

R: of what makes

S : India nationalism

(a) QSPR (b) QRSP (c) PQRS (d) QPRS

7. P : The fact is that

Q : Hindi is not spoken

R: of Indians

S : by a majority

(a) PQSR (b) RSPQ (c) PQRS (d) RSQP

8. P : another fact is

   Q: that UP does not

   R : represent the

   S : majority of India

   (a) PRSQ (b) SRQP (c) PQRS (d) QSRP

Transformation of Sentences

Select the option which transforms the given sentence without changing its meaning.

1. It is said that I am ruined.
   (a) Alas ! I am ruined.
   (b) Am I ruined?
   (c) It was said that I have been ruined.
   (d) I have been ruined.
2. It is very cruel of him.
   (a) How cruel of himself!
   (b) How cruel of him!
   (c) What cruel of him!
   (d) Alas! How cruel of him!
3. Being dissatisfied, he resigned.
   (a) He was dissatisfied yet he resigned.
   (b) He was dissatisfied and he resigned.
   (c) He was dissatisfied, so he resigned.
   (d) He being dissatisfied, he resigned.
4. Hearing the noise, the boy woke up.
   (a) The boy heard the noise and he woke up.
   (b) The boy heard the noise but he woke up.
   (c) The boy heard the noise because he woke up.
   (d) The boy heard the noise, so he woke up.

5. He must not be late to avoid punishment.
   (a) In the event of being late, he will be punished.
   (b) In the event of been late, he will be punished.
   (c) In the event of late, he will be punished.
   (d) In the event of being late, he can be punished.
6. Seeing the lion, he ran away.
   (a) He saw the lion but ran away.
   (b) He saw the lion but it ran away.
   (c) He saw the lion but he ran away.
   (d) He saw the lion and he ran away.
7. Walk carefully to avoid falling.
   (a) Walk carefully, so you will fall.
   (b) Walk carefully, otherwise you should fall.
   (c) Walk carefully, otherwise you will fall.
   (d) Walk carefully and you will not fall.
8. Now you are apparently tired.
   (a) Now you appears to be tired.
   (b) Now do you appear to be tired.
   (c) Now you appear to be tired.
   (d) Now you can appear to be tired.

ANSWERS TO CHECK POINTS

WORKSHEET 1

1. (a) am (b) carries (c) is (d) cannot
   (e) comes (f) has found (g) has performed
   (h) are gossiping and whiling away (i) keeps
   (j) creates, writes
2. (a) are (b) am (c) is (d) have
   (e) is (f) have been trying (g) do not know
   (h) cannot fix

WORKSHEET 14

1. (a) was still working (b) fell (c) were going
   (d) burnt (e) was waiting (f) had harvested
   (g) had fought, attained (h) had departed
2. (a) was brought up (b) has been working
   (c) heard (d) has been staying
   (e) broke, was dancing (f) had given
   (g) has not written (h) rang, was having

WORKSHEET 15

1. (a) wants (b) will operate (c) will stay
   (d) will win (e) will start (f) will have corrected
   (g) will certainly get (h) will have finished
2. (a) will have left (b) have arrived
   (c) will have ended (d) will start
   (e) will probably assign (f) will have finished
   (g) be completing (h) will have passed
3. (a) were driving (b) saw (c) thought
   (d) has been

ANSWERS TO EXAM PRACTICE

Error Correction

1. (d) No correction
2. (c) rains, will
3. (a) contributing
4. (d) No correction
5. (b) become
6. (b) is waiting
7. (c) have
8. (a) get
9. (d) No correction
10. (c) managing
11. (a) put
12. (b) has
13. (c) have been reading
14. (d) No correction
15. (b) had left
16. (d) No correction

17. (c) are leading
18. (c) was watching
19. (a) revolves
20. (a) had

Editing Tasks

1.

Incorrect	**Correct**
(a) has	had
(b) complete	completed
(c) is	was
(d) come	came
(e) will	would
(f) shall	would
(g) burnt	burn
(h) check	checked

2.

Incorrect	**Correct**
(a) meeting	met
(b) bring	brought
(c) were	was
(d) has	had
(e) are	is
(f) gave	gives
(g) live	living
(h) eats	eat

Omission Task

Before	**Missing**	**After**
(a) bookshop	is	not
(b) you	find	in
(c) which	were	once
(d) years	are	fading
(e) which	is	the
(f) he	has	read

(g) will	be	baffled
(h) just	read	his

Reordering of Sentences

1. (a) PRQS	2. (b) QPRS	3. (a) SPQR
4. (c) QSPR	5. (b) PQRS	6. (d) QPRS
7. (a) PQSR	8. (c) PQRS	

Transformation of Sentences

1. (a) Alas! I am ruined.
2. (b) How cruel of him!
3. (c) He was dissatisfied, so he resigned.
4. (d) The boy heard the noise, so he woke up.
5. (a) In the event of being late, he will be punished.
6. (d) He saw the lion and he ran away.
7. (c) Walk carefully, otherwise you will fall.
8. (c) Now you appear to be tired.

More to Learn

The simple past Tense form of a verb and the one used in the present perfect Tense may or may not be the same. Look at the table below –

Present Tense	Past Tense	Present Perfect
Clean	Cleaned	Has/have cleaned
Push	Pushed	Has/have pushed
Feel	Felt	Has/have felt
Sleep	Slept	Has/have slept
Tell	Told	Has/have told
Do	Did	Has/have done
Buy	Bought	Has/have bought
Break	Broke	Has/have broken
Speak	Spoke	Has/have spoken
Forget	Forgot	Has/have forgotten
Write	Wrote	Has/have written
Fall	Fell	Has/have fallen

Present Tense	Past Tense	Present Perfect
Clean	Cleaned	has/have cleaned
push	pushed	has/have pushed
feel	felt	has/have felt
sleep	slept	has/have slept
tell	told	has/have told
do	did	has/have done
go	went	has/have gone
buy	bought	has/have bought
break	broke	has/have broken
speak	spoke	has/have spoken
forget	forgot	has/have forgotten
write	wrote	has/have written
fall	fell	has/have fallen
see	saw	has/have seen
eat	ate	has/have eaten
drink	drank	has/have drunk
sink	sank	has/have sunk
begin	began	has/have begun

Look at the table below for examples of verbs that form the past Tense differently.

Present Tense	Past Tense	
See	Saw	Seen
Ride	Rode	Ridden
Leave	Left	Left
Come	Came	Come
Go	Went	Gone
Shut	Shut	Shut
Cut	Cut	Cut
Put	Put	Put
Dig	Dug	Dug
Draw	Drew	Drawn

Present Tense	Past	
Fly	Flew	Flown
Grow	Grew	Grown
Fight	Fought	Fought
Buy	Bought	Bought
Catch	Caught	Caught
Hide	Hid	Hidden
Bite	Bit	Bitten
Wake	Woke	Woken
Speak	Spoke	Spoken
Steal	Stole	Stolen

Present Tense	Past Tense	
Tell	Told	Told
Sell	Sold	Sold
Fall	Fell	Fallen
Deal	Dealt	Dealt
Mean	Meant	Meant
Drive	Drove	Driven
Read	Read	Read
Lead	Led	Led
Feed	Fed	Fed
Win	Won	Won

Practice

A. Fill in the blanks with the right form of the verbs in brackets.

1. We ____________ in Patna. Uncle Somesh ____________ us often. (live, visit)
2. I____________ apples. He ____________ mangoes. (like)
3. The shop __________ at noon and ________ open till midnight. (open, stay)
4. A postman ____________ letters. Doctors ____________ patients. (deliver, treat)
5. Monkeys are __________from one branch to the next. (jump)
6. Raman ____________ up early and ______________ for a walk. (wake, go)
7. Grandma is ______________ groceries. I am ____________ them. (buy, carry)
8. Isha ____________ to school. Her brother __________ by bus. (cycle, come)

B. Tick the right form of the verb to complete the sentences.

1. I am try/trying to open the jar. Please help/helping me.
2. Josh is goes/going to Chennai. He goes/going there every month.
3. Sudha snores/snoring in her sleep. She is not snores/snoring now.
4. Amit plays/playing in the park every day. He is not plays/playing there this week.
5. Birds make/making nests in trees. A mynah is make/making a nest in a flowerpot!
6. Asif is writes/writing a book these days. He usually writes/writing in the morning.
7. Tigresses teach/teaching their cubs to hunt. These cubs are learn/learning to hunt.
8. Prita and her friends are watch/watching birds. She is take/taking their pictures. She travels/travelling to forests every year. She is visit/visiting Ranthambore in Rajasthan for a week.

C. Complete the sentences with the right form of the verbs in brackets. The first one has been done for you.

1. Amit has *gone* to school. I am *going* there now. (go)
2. I have ______ to Ajay. I am _____ to the Isha now. (speak)
3. Seema has _________ to you. Are you ___________ to her now? (write)
4. The cat has __________ the cake. I am __________ a new one. (eat, bake)
5. Tommy has _________ two inches. Brownie is not ________ at all. (grow)
6. I have _________ a box. What are you __________ ? (buy)
7. Shiza is ___________ . Has she ____________her work? (leave, do)

D. Fill in the blanks with the right form of the verbs in brackets. Also use has or have.

1. We ______________________________ the clothes. (wash)
2. They __________________________ the competition. (win)
3. I ______________________________ pretty flowers. (paint)
4. They ________________________________ the salad. (eat)
5. I ______________________________ the answers. (write)
6. Alisha _____________________________ you not to cook today. (tell)
7. I _____________________________ a golden cat with black stripes. (see)
8. He _____________________ the groceries and I __________ ____________________________ the house. (bring, clean)

Practice

A. Underline the verbs in the simple past tense.

Talib was hungry. He went to the kitchen and opened the fridge. He took the milk out and heated it. Then he poured the milk into a tumbler and added some sugar and chocolate powder. He stirred the milk till it was dark brown.

Talib returned to his room. He picked up a book and began to read. He dipped a biscuit in the hot milk and let it melt in his mouth. Then he sipped the milk.

Dogs barked outside. A postman rang a neighbour's doorbell. A squirrel squeaked and ran away from a cat. Talib was lost in his book. He didn't hear a thing!

B. Write the simple past tense of the following verbs.

1. dig ____________
2. grow ____________
3. catch ____________
4. steal ____________
5. draw ____________
6. ride ____________
7. leave ____________
8. hide ____________
9. feed ____________
10. fall ____________

C. Fill in the blanks with the past continuous tense of the verbs in the brackets. Don't forget to add was or were.

1. Anita ____________ to school when I gave her a ride. (walk)
2. A cheetah ____________ a hare but could not catch it. (chase)
3. Niray __________________________ a book last night. (read)
4. We ______________ a bike when we had an accident. (ride)
5. The sun ______________________ as we reached home. (set)
6. Hundreds of women ___________ saris in the village. (weave)
7. A toad ___________ towards a pond when a snake ate it. (hop)
8. Nishat and I _______________ when the teacher saw us. (talk)
9. Saba and Amal _______________ at the edge of a jungle. (were) They _______________________________ in trees and bushes and then ____ each other. (play, hide, chase)
10. Last evening, Father ___________________________ and Mother _____________________________ directions. I ____________________ out of the window. (drive, give, look)

D. Make sentences in the past continuous tense. One has been done for you.

1. A grasshopper plays a guitar. Some ants carry food.

A grasshopper was playing a guitar. Some ants were carrying food.

2. The moon shines in the sky. Owls hoot in the trees.

____

3. A ship sails in the sea. Seagulls sit on its mast.

____

4. Wasim bowls to Rahul. The umpires watch carefully.

____

5. They fish in the river. They cast their net wide. Otters swim around the net.

____

____

Practice

A. Fill in the blanks with will or shall.

1. ________________ you help me carry the boxes, please?
2. The phone is ringing. ________________ I answer it?
3. They ________________________ win the contest next year.
4. He _____________________________ meet you next week.
5. The bird __________________________ feed its chicks.
6. She _______________________ not take a holiday this year.
7. ______________________ we go to the museum this evening?
8. The bus ________________ arrive at 5 o'clock in the morning.
9. The birds are thirsty. ____________ I give them some water?
10. You seem tired. ______________ you go to bed early today?

B. Tick the right word.

1. Will/Shall I help you cross the road?
2. They will/shall go to the bakery in the evening.
3. You will/shall be in Chandigarh in November.
4. Will/Shall he scold me if I don't finish my work on time?
5. What will/shall you do if you come face-to-face with a lion?
6. It is very cold in here. Will/Shall I make some tea?
7. Will/Shall she reach the airport on time? Will/Shall I help her pack her bags?

Exceptions for Present Continuous Tense

A. The following verbs are not normally used in present continuous tense, on account of their meaning: -

- Verbs of perception or senses, e.g. see, hear, smell, notice, recognize etc.
- Verbs of appearance, e.g. appear, look, seem etc.
- Verbs of thinking, e.g. think, suppose, believe, agree, consider, forget, know, imagine, mean etc.
- Verbs of emotion, e.g. want, wise, desire, feel, love, prefer etc.
- have, own, possess, be (except when used in the passive).

B. Change in Tenses: -

- ♦ If the reporting verb is in the present or the future tense, the tense of the reported speech is not changed:
  Satish says, "I am flying a kite."
  Satish says that he is flying a kite.
  Satish will say, "I want a glass of milk."
  Satish will say that he wants a glass of milk.
- ♦ If the reporting verb is in the past tense, then the tense of the reported speech will change as follows:

Direct		Indirect
Simple present	changes into	Simple past
write		wrote
Present Progressive	changes into	Past Progressive
am/is/are writing		*was/were writing*
Present Perfect	changes into	Past Perfect
has written		*had written*
Simple Past	changes into	Past Perfect
wrote		*had written*
Past Progressive	changes into	Past Perfect Progressive
was/were writing		*had been writing*

- ♦ If the direct speech expresses a historical fact, a universal truth or a habitual fact, then the tense of the direct speech will not change:

Direct : He said, "Honesty is the best policy."

Indirect : He said that honesty is the best policy.

Direct : He said, "The sun rises in the east."

Indirect : He said that the sun rises in the east.

Direct : Rakesh said, "I am an early riser."

Indirect : Rakesh said that he is an early riser.

Direct : She said, "God is omnipresent."

Indirect : She said that God is omnipresent.

Direct : The teacher said, "The First World War started in 1914."

Indirect : The teacher said that the First World War started in 1914.

C. Direct and Indirect Speech

The words spoken by a person can be reported in two ways—Direct and Indirect. When we quote the exact words spoken by a person, we call it Direct Speech.

- Sohan said to Mohan, "I am going to school."

The exact words spoken by Sohan are put within inverted commas. But when we give the substance of what Sohan said, it is called Indirect Speech.

Sohan told Mohan that he (Sohan) was going to school.

1. Reporting Clause and Reported Speech:

Sohan told Mohan that he was going to school. The words which generally come before the inverted commas are called the reporting clause, i.e. Sohan said to Mohan and the verb 'said', is called the reporting verb. The words spoken by Sohan and put within inverted commas are called the reported speech, i.e. "I am going to school."

2. Rules for Changing Direct Speech into Indirect Speech:

- In the Indirect Speech, no inverted commas are used.
- The conjunctions that, if, whether, are generally used after the reporting verb.
- The first word of the reported speech begins with a capital letter.
- The tense of the reporting verb is never changed.
- The reporting verb changes according to sense: it may be told, asked, inquired.

3. Rules for the Change of Pronouns:

- The first person pronouns (I, me, my, we, us, our) in the reported speech change according to the subject of the reporting verb.
- The pronouns of the second person (you, your, yourself) in the reported speech change according to the object of the reporting verb.
- The pronouns of the third person do not change.

For example:

1. He said, "I like the book."
   He said that he liked the book.
2. He said to me, "Do you like the book?"
   He asked me if I liked the book.
3. He said, "He likes the book."
   He said that he liked the book.
4. Changes in words expressing nearness, time, auxiliaries, etc.

this	changes into	that
these	changes into	those
now	changes into	then
here	changes into	there
today	changes into	that day
tomorrow	changes into	the next day
yesterday	changes into	the previous day
last night	changes into	the previous night
can	changes into	could
may	changes into	might
shall	changes into	should
will	changes into	would
ago	changes into	before
just	changes into	then
come	changes into	go
thus	changes into	so

D. There has been a burglary. Inspector Kamat is asking some questions.

What was happening in the house last evening between 7 and 8 pm?

I think I was cooking. No, I am sorry, I was watching a movie. My husband was talking to his friend. My son was driving home. My grandchildren were playing carrom. Their mother was getting ready to go out. Our dog was sleeping.

The verbs in blue tell us what was going on during a particular time in the past. These sentences are in the past continuous tense. Was and were are used as helping verbs in these sentences. We use the -ing form of verbs to show that something was or is happening.

One can simply add -ing to the simplest form of most verbs to make their -ing forms. Some verbs form their -ing forms differently. Look at the rules below.

1. In some verbs that end with -e, we drop the e and add -ing.

bite	biting
hide	hiding
rise	rising
breathe	breathing

dance	dancing
weave	weaving
write	writing
ride	riding

live	living
change	changing
graze	grazing
cycle	cycling